Short Stories for Thought and Wonder

Avonelle Kelsey

ISBN: 978-1-957532-19-6

Cover design by Nola Lee Kelsey

Soggy Nomad Press
6960 N 5th St.
North Las Vegas, NV 89084

SoggyNomadPress.com

Table of Contents

PAGING DR. FREUD

"Paging Dr. Freud, Paging Dr. Freud..." The paging system in heaven was heard by no one but the person for whom the message was intended, however, it was an inauspicious time to interrupt.

"There?... Oh, yes... Just right and ahaaaa." Then deep sighs were the only answer the pager received.

"Paging Dr. Freud. Doctor, are you still screwing around with Helen of Troy? For God's sake, get yourself to the palace at once. This is an emergency."

"Pardon me, Helen, my Dear. Jesus is calling. Guess he's worried about his Father again." She looked at him questioningly, but Dr. Freud did not indulge the confidences of his patients.

He bowed and kissed her hand, "Thank you for sharing a Trojan experience with me. So many men have chosen you as their fantasy figure, I just had to look you up and find out what the incomprehensible hold you have over men is."

"Now do you know?" she asked archly.

He looked at her pale oval face in the moonlight. Fine strands of red hair floated in the breeze across her naked body, full soft lips glistened moistly, eyes sparkled with life. The scent of her filled his nostrils and the siren voice beckoned. The measureless depths of feminine mystery lured him back. His desire rose again. She smiled.

For a brief moment, he knew why Odysseys roamed, why the Trojans and Achaeans of the earth warred with one another. Somewhere, within womanhood lay the secret security each man longs for but hasn't the capacity to decipher for himself. Helen was the personification, the symbolized form that could turn the key and lead mankind from Pandora's Box to a New Eden. If he could just understand the mystique.

"Sigmund. This is Jesus. You're keeping me waiting," came a frosty voice in his ear.

"Coming, Lord. Beam me up. Don't wait up, Helen," he bowed gallantly again and when he straightened up, he was in the presence of Jesus.

"Sorry, but I felt I had just discovered the secret we've been looking for, when you called me."

"Good. You'd better have. You've been researching for a century. Sometimes it's confusing, even to me, whether the subject is sex or war."

"Perhaps. . . What's the emergency?"

"Some fool has his finger on The Red Button ready to destroy the Earth.   God has put everything in limbo temporarily and I'm trying to stop him from giving up the whole earthy experiment."

"Is it the masculine or feminine aspect of God that wants to quit?"

"The malefactor of Father/God of course. It was the Mother/God side that saved it the last time, sending me with a message to say that caring and understanding would bring the completion of love, in other words, would solve most of their problems."

He shook his head thoughtfully, then continued, "I was misquoted so often the meaning became distorted. Apparently, it didn't take anyway. Father wants to throw up his hands, feed the whole solar system to a Black Hole Garbage Disposal after one big bang and go on to other things." He grinned to cover his feeling of failure.

"Mother says he must see it through. That he hasn't given my experiment enough time and energy. Suddenly, he's decided to turn the whole Earth over to me and I'm not certain where to start. You're the greatest Psychologist mankind has produced, unless maybe Jung. If you don't have any solutions to the nature of Earth's problems, perhaps he will have some."

Freud grinned widely. He had not expected Jesus to stoop to blackmail.

Jesus smiled slightly then burst into laughter at himself. The whole of heaven lit up. In his heart, Sigmund felt the torch of love. Here was another clue.

Jesus said, "I'm sorry to be so impatient. Apparently, you have things you wish to talk with me about. He grabbed a passing cloud and stretched out on it. Freud followed suit and sat in the refreshing mist across from him.

Around them a million different sunsets changed the colors of the clouds and their surroundings every few minutes. Sweet fragrant odors filled the air. Singing and laughter hovered in the background. All the wonderful things and beings that had ever happened on the earth were stored about them and implored Freud and Jesus to save them.

"I haven't the answers, but I have some possibilities that we can think about, if you will let me refresh our memories and build on them?"

"You have the cloud, Doctor." Jesus smiled at his own pun.

"As I recall: In the beginning was energy. This core of masculine/feminity was embodied in what mankind later called God. God felt compressed and decided to expand. This created a big bang and the Universe spun out in a fascinating array of various hunks of matter. For the fun of it, God lit many of them. These suns gave brightness and color to the matter.

"However, these massive pieces were forever banging into one another and breaking up. It was fun for awhile, like the fourth of July in New York City.

"Finally, God decided to regulate things a bit. By the use of gravitational and magnetic forces, it became pretty well organized. He set up a few black holes for garbage disposal, to collect the mass back into the original energy as bits and pieces ran the course of time and disintegrated. Nothing is ever really lost completely.

"So that it didn't become too stagnant, he left some things to chance. This one bit of instability may be fun to a God, but to primitive mankind, chance may have lead to his downfall."

"How so?"

"I believe the big four-letter word people most hate to admit to feeling is called FEAR. When God began to sculpt the amoebae, then get more complicated with fishes, plants, birds and animals, their natures blended with that of the planet. Everything was adapted to the random laws and to accepting passively, whatever nature put in their way." Jesus nodded somewhat impatiently.

"That is, until God designed man. Your Mother/God part was playing with another dimension, so right away, a 'male only' put things a bit out of balance. Added to the fact that this strange new creature was not only more intelligent but more fragile than any other animal. In fact, he was so fragile that God put him in a protected area called the Garden of Eden. For awhile he wandered around and had a great time, but something was missing.

"God had put the key to complete maturity and the gate to the outside world, in the fruits of the Tree of Knowledge and Life. The man didn't seem too interested in it. The lower fruits were to be eaten first, God had thought by the time the upper ones were eaten, man would be ready for the key to universal secrets such as knowledge of life, love, the metamorphose of death, but most of all, a thorough understanding of Man's own nature. He would be able to function in the world outside the Garden in much the same way as a God."

"That is all past history, Doctor. Can't you move along faster?" Jesus asked.

"Not really. As I speak, so I think, then act. That is man's nature. As you think, so you act. That is your nature."

"Ok, take your time. I'm listening."

"When your Mother/God side was finally consulted, she quickly said, "He needs a loving companion.""

"Now God had a bit more experience when he made the female and he made her more delicately beautiful and of a more loving nature, more feminine, less animalistic. She was more curious and different from Adam, more flexible. Her body was soft and inviting. It would in time, when she matured, be fruitful and multiply. Her babies as well as her husband would find comfort in its bumps and curves. The animalistic tendencies were more deeply buried in her nature, but they were still there... I've always wondered why she was called Eve," he said musingly.

"Oh," Jesus said, "That was Adam's idea. Adam called her Eve because he slept one afternoon until almost dark. When he awoke from dreaming, she stood before him. The setting sun painted her body orange. She was small and lovely to behold, all gift-wrapped in a sunset. They looked at one another for the first time. The first human female..." He broke off and for a moment forgot their previous discussion.

Freud found it fascinating that Jesus could be caught up in a fantasy about a woman and wondered if he too had sexual dreams.

Jesus continued, "God said, 'This is woman. She will be your companion when I am not with you.'

"Adam was content when woman came into the Garden. He wasn't particularly interested in gaining more insight and knowledge, except when he sensed the woman's restlessness and wanted to impress her. For the most part,

Eve, God, fishing, naming and exploring kept him busy. Eve was strange to the earth and Adam took great pleasure in showing off by giving things and places names just as God had named him." Again Jesus paused and Freud took over.

"At first she enjoyed the lovely trees, Adam and exploring. But as she began to mature into a woman, she too became restive.

Eve was curious about the Tree of Life and the rainbow dew drops that hung on ' iridescent petaled leaves. She often sat under it and looked through the gate at the animals and their babies. The snake usually accompanied her when Adam was off with God or fishing. He often wished God would make a woman for him.

"One day he climbed up high in the tree above her and inadvertently knocked a piece of the higher fruit down. She picked up the organic computer chip which was much the same shape and color as an Apple. God had told Adam about the tree but hadn't said too much to Eve.

"Adam had repeated God's words, that we would die to this place if we ate of the fruit before our time," Eve quoted these words, turning the strange fruit back and forth in the sunlight.

"'Ye shall not surely die. Where else is there? Have you ever seen anything die here in Eden?' He asked.

"Snake was curious too. He had been in The Garden since its creation. Neither of them knew much about dying.

"Eve tasted the fruit. It was delicious. Before she could take another bite, Adam arrived hungry. She readily reached the apple to him to taste and he ate all of it."

Freud shook his head sadly, "The male side of God itself knew little of forgiveness. He did not let them die, but turning two immature people out into the hostile atmosphere of the Earth was certainly a punishment. In psychological terms I would say, 'The punishment did not fit the crime.'

"Mankind is still paying the price of being curious and trying to use the God-given mind for something other than passive obedience. Chance was challenged but it overwhelmed the immature beings and they were not only ashamed of their nakedness, but of their lack of knowledge about themselves and the world into which they were cast.

"In other words, they were afraid of nearly everything. A bit of paranoia has been passed from generation to generation to the present day. Like the children they are, they reach for security in things, be it rocks, more than others, or weapons.

"Your man with the finger on the button is full of fear. His only security at the moment is the power he feels as he lowers his finger and thumbs his nose at a God who dared to make a weakling like him."

Freud could see Jesus begin to get interested in what he was saying. He continued.

"Eve's body was still that of a child in many ways. It has never fully matured in any woman. That is why no human baby is ever born mature like that of most animals. If she survives the first birth, she becomes a slave to the child for many years to come. The man may or may not take responsibility.

"It depends upon how enticing she makes herself, or how stringent the pseudo-priests make the laws for society to take care of its own. For survival, the woman has had to cultivate mystique. It too hides fear." Jesus nodded thoughtfully as he recalled the mystique and insecurity of the women he had known on earth.

"The human brain, with all its potential, does not get a chance to mature. Parents, trained by untrained parents and educators, keep the cycle of immaturity and lack of self-awareness going. Because people do not know and accept themselves as worthy of becoming as Gods, in other words, meet their potential, they subvert, submit and close their eyes in fear.

"They become a collector of things in order to feel secure. When a group or person becomes powerful enough by collecting more than the rest of the people, they still feel insecure and often begin wars to get more. The masses fall in line with it because, temporarily, they too have goals and a possibility of obtaining more security. If they keep their eyes straight ahead, for awhile, their fears dissolve. They rape, plunder, kill and steal, in the name of God, religion, some Country, King or Queen. They see people looking toward them with attention. Someone really sees them and may not walk blindly over them, is the main reason the average person goes to war... Men need self-confidence in themselves...in life before chance cuts the ground from under them...if they could know what each other is thinking, they would not have to fear dishonesty. Maybe an increase in the magnetic field would strengthen brain waves, honesty would bring self-confidence as fear dissolved.

Jesus stirred restlessly on his cloud and sat up, his breath increased with excitement, "Yes... yes..."

"So, you're saying that if we take away chance, people will not be afraid, but then they will be bored. Sounds like a double-bind to me."

"A real Catch-22, Jesus. But I have some ideas that we might carry out in an experimental way, if we can return to earth and stall for time."

"You name it, I'll take care of it," Jesus said eagerly.

"First, we need a miracle for the guy with his finger hovering above the button. What could change his mind? Any ideas, Sigmund?" Jesus asked.

"Well, Helen of Troy was not busy when I saw her last."

ABORIGINAL RETRIBUTION

Baboloon peered into the gaping maw of a steep-sided volcanic cone. Green scum and water lilies covered the surface several hundred feet below. He shuddered and muttered, "Devil, Devil Hole."

This was the dreaded punishment arena, especially for women. It was the hole Aborigines threw women into when they dared disobey their husbands, or refused to abide by tribal rules.

There were tales that the place was haunted, that after a woman was thrown in, she could be heard singing along with the fierce wind that roared around the top at night. Sometimes eerie lights flickered below and voices could be heard calling. Few were brave enough to linger in the dark. After a sacrifice, the tribe usually raced down the trail and away from the evil spot.

Usually, when a man committed a crime, he was allowed to stand before his judge with a shield and dodge anything the relatives of the wronged persons chose to throw at him, for as long as they wished. Sometimes a man was lucky enough to survive. Even then, he was often forced to become an outcast like Baboloon. But not so, the women. The Devil, Devil Hole waited for them with it's gaping maw.

Now Baboloon was larger and stronger than the average man in his tribe. He took pride in his strength and was envied by many of the males. Because of his size and handsomeness, the women were easily taken in by his charms. Sometimes, the men ganged up on him in jealous anger. In retaliation, he seduced their women.

For a time, they were relieved from the pressure of his potency when Baboloon fell in love with the beautiful Sheileen and took her for his wife. For a short time, all was blissful. But man is a creature of habit. Baboloon could not remain faithful. When a woman passed in front of him, his eyes followed each sinuous movement.

Sheileen soon learned of his affairs. "I want you to be faithful to me," Sheileen shouted in anger and jealousy, then sobbed. "Do you want another wife?"

Baboloon took her in his arms. The large man wanted to deny is unfaithfulness. He wanted to be faithful but he had given into impulsive desires so often. He tried to explain,

"Other than the moment, the women were. . .well, wonderful. It is only you I wish for a wife."

"The other men complain when you seduce their wives and daughters. The women will not talk to me." Her tears fell like raindrops on her ebony cheeks. On their love pallet of grass and leaves, he dried her tears and promised to remain faithful. But, each time a woman walked by his eyes continued to followed and soon, his body.

After several stormy scenes, Sheileen closed her robes and withdrew her laughter and passion from him. It was the first woman's right to accept or reject her husband's unfaithfulness. She could choose a woman as a wife or send him from her hut. However, Baboloon did not lust after just one woman, but many.

The tribal council said, "She is justified in sending him away." They were especially supportive of Sheileen since the other women he seduced were their daughters, sisters, and they often suspected, their own wives. Too many new born babies looked more like Baboloon than their own fathers. The men were happy for an excuse to rid the tribe of this competition.

Sheileen refused to have Baboloon stand in front of a shield to be stoned, but turned her eyes and walked away from him to stand behind the tribe council while they announced the verdict.

"From this day forward, you are no longer a member of our tribe. You are a trouble maker Baboloon. If we see you again, we will kill you. Go away! Leave Sheileen and the tribe in peace," the Chief commanded.

Baboloon looked pleadingly at Sheileen. She turned her back to him.

After this, the members of his tribe drove him away anytime he approached their encampment.

Baboloon's longing for Sheileen became stronger with passing time. It became so great that he was no longer satisfied with other women. He became so obsessed he felt he would die if he could not have her. Often he followed the tribe at a distance, as he had today, hoping to find Sheileen alone and run away with her.

Her new man, Tjapukai, collected a group of warriors and often chased him through the rainforest with spears raised, shouting "Kill, kill."

He had been able to cover his trail. They gave up the search each time, but continued to remained alert.

Sadly, he turned back down the trail, walking away from the Devil Devil Hole to the waterfall below. Baboloon was so lonely. He sighed regretfully as he remembered the passionate nights and comfort he had found in the arms of Sheileen.

The noise from the waterfall at the foot of the volcanic cone, Devil Devil Hole, was deafening as the fifty foot stream plunged with a thunderous roar, leaping joyfully into the air, twisting and turning as its droplets danced downward to become prancing foam. Then, each spread out, meekly composing themselves into a rich green pond, all calm and tranquil on the surface.

Baboloon caught his breath. On the edge of the waterfall sat Sheileen, alone. She sat without moving, as though waiting and dreaming of some past mysterious knowledge. To Baboloon, in his deep longing, she was now the perfect, unattainable woman. Remote, mystical, impervious to past events. She must be waiting for him.

There had been a time when he had been able to break through her enigmatic calm, but he had destroyed the gift of innocent vulnerability by treating it lightly and abusing her expectations.

"If could get her alone, I know I could make her love me again," he muttered. He told himself she waited for him as she had so often in the past. Her breasts were more rounded and body fuller than he remembered. Could she be carrying his child? His heart quickened. He must have her.

Cunningly, he looked about. Then he followed her gaze. In a distance the tribe gathered around two, fighting, male tree kangaroos. Their spears were raised. Both kangaroos would be losers. One would give in and scramble away. The winner would become the tribe's evening meal.

Baboloon rested his spear against a tree. Quietly he stole to the bank of the pool and slipped into the water. He swam up behind the rock on which Sheileen perched. Before she could scream, he pulled her into the water and swam with her to the edge of the pool. With one hand clamped across her mouth, he pulled her quickly up the edge, threw her over his shoulder and slipped into the jungle.

Tjapukai glanced up just in time to see Baboloon pick up his spear and disappear into the rainforest with Sheileen over his shoulder. Giving a warning shout, he called the other warriors.

Baboloon did not know he had been spotted. He found a soft bed of moss, lay his struggling beloved upon it and satisfied himself for the moment. Soon he would make her love him again She lay back with frightened eyes and looked over his shoulder.

Baboloon glanced upward. The tribe had surrounded them. Tjapukai was raising his spear above his head ready to plunge it into Baboloon. He rolled off Sheileen. The spear missed, sinking into the heart of his beloved.

Without thinking, Baboloon kept rolling and dodging spears. He began to run, pausing when he heard the anguished wail from Tjapukai. Sheileen had received the spear meant for him, he realized. Baboloon lifted his voice to join Tajapukai's in one long wail.

After a time he decided they were not following him and crept back in the direction he had come. Baboloon kept in the shadows and followed closely behind the tribe when he spotted the procession. Sheileen was being carried around the waterfalls and up the path toward the volcanic cone. Even in death she was still to be punished. Stoically, Tjapukai threw Sheileen over the edge.

Then, with a loud roar the tribe set out as one to find Baboloon and kill him. They spread out. He retreated. Tajapukai spotted his trail. Suddenly, he realized he was caught between the Devil Devil Hole and the warriors. Baboloon backed up the trail.

There was no way around the volcanic cone. The only place the tops of the sharp rocks could be approached was on the sacrificial ledge. Many women had taken their last breath as they plunged into it's mysterious green depths.

Now, it was Baboloon's time. Either he jumped or died with a body full of spears. He hesitated on the ledge. Then, with one last wail for Sheileen, he dived off the edge of the cliff into the depths of the green water far below.

Baboloon's body plunged down, down into the arms of the green death that awaited him. His lungs nearly burst. Finally, his body paused and shot upwards.

As he reached the surface, hands grabbed him from behind and pulled him toward a cavern ledge. He coughed and gasped for air. They lay him face down across a rock with his feet still in the water. Finally, he was able to lift his head and look at his surroundings..

The body of Sheileen was lying nearby in a bed of red blossoms.

Women of all ages, sizes and shapes were gathered around him in front of a large opening which ran a long way back into a cavern. Sunlight filtered through small openings high overhead. Gardens of food and flowers bloomed everywhere. The women wore only flowers.

In spite of the pain in his chest, Baboloon smiled triumphantly when he realized the wonderful situation into which he had fallen. He could not believe his luck as he looked at the women. But, there were no smiles of welcome. A vague uneasiness tugged at his mind.

The spear which had been in the body of Sheileen was in the hand of a large strong woman. She nodded.

Suddenly, his hands were tied with a willow thong. Before he could stand up, his feet were tied, also. He was rolled over onto his back. The large woman with a spear came toward him, raising it above her head, ready to stab him in the heart.

An older woman cried out. "Wait, wait," she said and pointed at his erection which had begun at the fear of death.

One woman asked, "Why do you stop? All men must die."

Another said, "We have been blessed to be away from men. They made us slaves and used up our bodies with too many children, diseases and abuse."

"Aiii, death to men." They shouted in chorus.

The old woman held up her hand. "But, what is the one thing we have missed which they had to give us?"

"Babies," several of them said at once.

"That is true," said the older women.

"The other men who have been thrown over have been dead," another said musingly.

"But it is men who have always been so cruel to us. We agreed that any living man who might come, would be killed."

"Ah, yes. That is also true," said the wise woman. "But, let us each receive the only gift worth receiving from a man before we kill him. When the babies are born, one strong male child will be allowed to remain alive until each woman has a child. When all the women who wish to be impregnated have been satisfied, he will be sacrificed as we have been."

"Aiii." they shouted.

"It is agreed then. We keep him alive until each of us is pregnant?"

"Aiiiii," the shout went up again as they gathered around Baboloon.

He felt the many lustful hands on his body which automatically reacted sexually to their seductive touching.

He writhed and shuddered. Their demands were relentless. When he was drained and their demands met, they lay him by his beloved Sheileen in a dark corner far back in the cavern.

There are many ways to die!

FAIRYLAND

"Now quit that," I said wiggling down under the silken sheet covering my head. "I'm still asleep."

Ripple and Jazz, my two male lovers on this scintillating planet, dived under the blanket with me and began to nibble my ears and chirp an enchanting love-making melody.

"Hey, cut that out. You wore me out last night. That's why I'm still in bed. What do you want?" I was both surprised and flattered. Usually they played around during the dark of the suns and rested in the caverns in early morning when the suns were brightest...

I envied the handsome creatures that lived on this enchanting planet which we had named Aerie or Fairyland. It was the most beautiful place we astronauts had visited thus far. Everything on it was light and airy. The gravity let even my clumsy body soar through the air for several yards at a time.

When we first landed, the inhabitants had to hold us down and teach us to glide as we rebounded at least ten feet with each step. It was fun. We laughed and they chirped, danced and giggled with us, until patiently, we could glide off a limb or jump like a Tarzan through the treetops and up from the ground.

It was a treat to be around a people with a sense of humor. They sang a little song as they taught us to maneuver on the surface of their planet.

"Just give a little wiggle, take a little jump, wave your arms, be a bird, run and hop...hip pity hop." They laughed and treated us like children, except when making love.

Ripple and Jazz had attached themselves to me from the first. Perhaps it was because I was so plain and my skin was dull in comparison to Christie's lustrous mane and radiant complexion. She had plenty of attention however, as did the rest of the crew. We were new and different. They were extremely intelligent and always bombarding us with questions.

"From where do you herald?"

"We call our planet Earth."

"Where is Earth?"

At first, we were reluctant to give the precise location of our planet, but these knowing people soon homed in on the location of our solar system. We were not certain they had a collective consciousness or an ESP form of communication, but it certainly seemed so at times.

Nearly everyone on the ship had fallen in love with an alien or two. Who could help it? They were full of fun, curiosity, and so lovely to see and touch. Their features seemed a bit more birdlike than ours, but it also gave them a strange exotic beauty. Under a microscope, their flesh was covered with tiny feathers; their bones were less dense than ours but seemed strong. The Aries hair was long and flowing. In flight it reminded me of wings. Their childlike love and innocence never failed to astonish us. Yet, of what had they to fear? They seemed perfectly adapted to their climate, whereas the earth was nearly always too hot or to cold for the naked body to accommodate. If they were childlike, I suspected that mentally, we were the infantile ones.

I was one of a team of thirteen astronauts assigned as ambassadors to explore our own galaxy. Usually our reception on a planet was met with silence, shyness, or sometimes hostility. Not so in Fairyland.

Even before we left our ship in orbit and descended, we were bombarded with messages and invited to visit. They even flew up in one of their own ship to inspect ours. This was a bit unusual, but they were so lovingly innocent that we bent the rules a bit.

The actual planets name was some musical sounding phrases like, Inchuswan-chi-arie. Their language was a cross between talking, whistling and singing. It wasn't too tough to learn, once I quit being so serious about it and played around. They had picked ours up readily but each sentence sounded like a song.

We loved the Aries and their planet from the beginning.

It seemed as thought everything on the surface twinkled, or was soft and pastel. Some of the hills were emeralds, topaz covered with vegetation, diamond gravel, gold and silver sand. The vegetation sparkled with dewdrops which tasted like honey. Rocks were often gold, pink quartz, and turquoise. The soil was lush and covered with grasses of many colors. Each color was tiny delicious pods of different flavors. To eat, one only had to bend over. Trees were hung with fruit all year round. Huge crystal caverns gushed with waterfalls and pools.

Whereas on Earth we valued sparkle and glitter, the Aerie or Feather People as we sometimes called them, sought out the dull and quiet of these inner caves. They loved our early Earth classical movies when we showed them entertainment from home and enjoyed acting them out.

"Where did you get such large, lovely feathers," I asked as Ripple and Jazz presented me with an armful much as an Earth lover presented roses.

"Let us show you," Jazz said bowing gallantly. "Better yet, let's take her for a ride," Ripple promptly gave a whistle. I could see he must be reaching a tone which I could not hear as his lips remained puckered. I heard an answering sound and a graceful feathered horse settled before us.

The feathers which they also wore as adornment came from this highly valued horse-bird which they bred like cattle. It was almost the size of an ostrich, but more heavily winged and feathered. They tamed them for low flying and short distances much as we ride horses on Earth. All of them tried at one time or another and wished we had such a species on our home planet.

Our geneticists wondered, "If we could cross them with a horse, we could have a truly fairy tale Pegasus." He was forever coming up with a new crossbreed. However, the captain didn't feel a space ship needed these creatures until we set up a trading route between the solar systems. We sent many picture back to Earth. To our surprise, they said that our holo transmissions were not very clear.

We received a call from Earth. "Why are you tarrying so long on the Aries Planet?"

"The extremely high intelligence of these people, their excellent health and their technology need to be studied in depth," our captain replied.

He loved the people as well and might have been afraid of a rebellion if he commanded us to leave too soon. We had been traveling for a long while and had both earned and needed some vacation time.

However, his statement was partially true. Their lightweight material, which was both flexible and endurable, was perfect for nearly any kind of vehicle, plane, house, tool or equipment they needed. So far, we had not found out the source of the ore used. It seemed to be somewhere between a plastic and flexible steel. A silken metal.

Since everything seemed to be kept in common centers and each person checked out what she or he needed, it was surprising how few vehicles, tools, etc. a society really used.

I loved their homes. They lived in bird cages or so we termed them, high up in the trees. These cages swung lightly in the gentle breeze that flowed across the face of the planet. Two suns kept it light about eighteen hours a day, which was nearly twenty-eight of our earth hours long.

They were like us in body, yet different. The Aries' skin had the ability to change shades. It rippled like Mother of Pearl, with each movement. They were fascinating to watch in the sunlight, or as they flew. I guess they didn't actually fly. The gravity was so light and their long slender bodies cast themselves up from the surface, or out of a tree, with the effortlessness of a bird.

Their love making, too, was like a game, with one, two or three, singing, stroking, doing a little dance around the room, or sometimes they danced us into the mysterious caverns behind waterfalls. But Ripple and Jazz seemed to find me fascinating and two partners were more than enough. I loved their attention and them. It was good to know I didn't have to make a choice.

They were seldom serious. Sometimes they seemingly gave out a lot of information that added up to very little in hard facts.

This morning they chirped, "We've something to show you that you've wanted to see. The Vigils finally gave us permission to take you to a special place." Ripple said, nibbling my toe.

"Course if you'd rather stay in bed," Jazz kissed my lips and curled his fingers in my hair.

"Ok, you win." They pulled me up and out of bed. Each roosting tree, or bird cage apartment house, had pipes that ran water out the limbs to the tops of the houses, regardless of how high up in the air they were. Since there was a great deal of moisture in the air and light rain daily, there was a collecting bowl on the top which usually provided enough water to take a shower. This smelled spicy, as did their whole atmosphere.

We astronauts wore very little clothing in space so we soon adopted their garmentless habit, especially as we learned to fly. Clothing impeded flight-walk. Often we carried light backpacks. None of the natives carried anything on them except bits of jewelry, feathers, etc. They had no money, almost no possessions and needed few since food was plentiful and furniture was organic as were the apartment homes. It was as though they trusted their environment to meet their needs and it did.

The Aries carved a pumpkin and gourd like fruit, or at the time we thought it was fruit, into many interesting shapes and sometimes added color. The apartment shapes were open on the sides and slated vertical blinds were use to let in air, block rain or shade different areas.

Their favorite topics of conversations were cross pollination.

"What plants do you have on your planet?"

I told them about Luther Burbank, Johnny Apple seed and genetics. Also, about weeds and cactus.

"It must be an unloving planet to grow plants which hurt people."

"There was once supposed to be a place called the Garden of Eden." I told them about the old Biblical story.

They looked at one another and nodded.

"What?" I knew they were sending thoughts to one another. Sometimes it was as though their thought communication made a little hum in my head. I could almost understand them. Were they deliberately tuning me out, I wondered. They scooped me up, tossed me into the air and took me to taste a new food seed.

The Aries enjoyed developing different plants and conforming them to their needs much as we do metal. If someone wanted to use something, like a vehicle, they checked it out or waited until the other person who had it was through with it. They always moved swiftly and gracefully but seemed to be in no hurry once they arrived.

"I wish I could take one of your houses back with me," I told them.

"Why not?" Ripple said, and then put his fingers to his lips.

Jazz said, "He's joking."

"But I'm not," I insisted. The cushions and couches in your homes are like plants with soft bark or large leaves that smell and feel luxurious. Even the floors are porous, dirt falls through."

"I thought you said you needed enclosed homes to keep out the wind and cold," Jazz reminded me.

"I know, but I can dream, can't I?"

Jazz smiled, kissed my lips and whispered, "Why dream when the real thing is waiting for your embrace."

Later, we met in a group and talked as we watched a sunset.

"Do you believe in God?" Christie asked the Aries.

"What is God?"

"You tell him, Lorna," Gordon commented. "You're always talking about meaning of life."

I looked about and said doubtfully, "Maybe God is needed where people are afraid and have to fight for survival. Here, food is free, the air is clean. You each do a small amount of work and have lots of time for fun and creativity. Maybe this is heaven." All of the astronauts laughed but for once the Aries were thoughtful.

We had admired their seemingly simple form of self-government. Each one worked about two hours per day checking regulation controls of water, manufacturing of light cells for building homes, and on some transport planes or vehicle repair. The population seemed to be strictly controlled in spite of their strong sexual appetites. They never over-ate their supply of food. I never saw any deaths. The group sat with their arms about the companion on either side and seemed to bask in silence.

I thought about our time here. For the first few weeks, we just enjoyed the first really relaxing vacation we had in the five years, since we had set out from earth to explore the galaxy.

However, it was past time to leave. Our captain had called a meeting for 1 o'clock, earth-time aboard; the ship's original launching hour. We were all thinking sadly of the moment of departure.

The tiny watch monitors which each of us had embedded just below the skin with the surface had a time face, as well as a communication device for use between one another and the ship. It monitored our body, outside temperature, and could even take a picture. We each knew there was a backup monitor hidden on board ship. This too collected information for the ships computer and sent messages directly to Earth.

The siren's of Odysseys might be waiting out there for us, was the logic from the central earth space programmers. There was also a capsule inside the devices for our destruction or just plain nausea which gave one the psychological feeling of wanting to get away from a situation.

Our captain was also a Psychiatrist. In our travels, all of us could control the ship but could we control ourselves? In any event, I must make that meeting.

"All right," I told Jazz and Ripple, "slow down. I'd love to go with you, but I have a command performance to be at the ship at one, or three hours from now in Fairyland time."

"We'll have you back in plenty of time. You've been wondering about our death and life cycles. We have received approval from the Collective and the Vigils to show you these. The Collective was their loosely formed central government, from what we could ascertain. I had not heard of the Vigils before and was curious, but decided not to question too much until later.

Resting was sleeping, of which they seemed to need little, since they took short cat naps off and on all day. They delighted in the few hours of semi-darkness when both suns had set. When we felt the greatest need to sleep, they were the most active.

"We'll take a transport so you can return in time. The location is over the border." This in itself was enticing.

Always before they had discouraged us from going far beyond the boundaries of their warm climate toward the poles. From the ship above we could ascertain some action such as light mining and people, but much of the work seemed to be done underground, not above it as in the Fairyland towns in which we stayed near the equator.

"Can Christie and Jordan go along?" I asked. The two communicated something over my heads. I could sense reluctance and then agreement.

You birds can't fool me for too long, I thought. You do have a form of ESP. I had been determined to find out more about it ever since we first arrived. When questioning them, they came up with something which sounded like 'high sound.' Something which our ears were not capable of hearing.

The light atmosphere seemed to be very conductive to any kind of waves, including brain waves. Christie, Jordan, and I had been carrying on experiments in it for years. We had been more successful on this planet, when we were not too far apart.

She was only a branch away so I closed my eyes and said, "Christie." For a moment I did not get an answer. Then I realized she was struggling up from sleep.

"Lorna?" she responded.

"Get ready to go with us." My energy ran out.

I missed phones so I tuned in my wrist node, and ran our voices through the ship's computer.

"Christie, Jordan, Jazz and Ripple have invited us to go to their final restrings over the borders. We have to leave right away if we want to be back for the meeting. They'll take a transport. We'll pick you up at the base in ten minutes." I tuned out. A frown appeared for the first time on the face of my friends.

Puzzled, I asked, "Is something wrong?"

"Well, we didn't want everyone to know that we were showing you our sacred place."

"Oh, I'm so sorry. But the crew won't bother us. We can't communicate as easily with our minds as you can, but we're learning."

They laughed. Often they had said it was as though our minds had calcified. Our thoughts flowed too slowly. I wondered if it made it more difficult for them to understand us and annoyed them. Everything seemed to come so easily in their world.

I remembered one time when I had been able to get some of the females apart. They talked more readily about the social structure than did the males.

An older one said she remembered a time when all was not as smoothly running on the planet as it was now. As a child, the Collective had taken over and declared childbearing naturally as unlawful. Now, each female spent the time necessary once a year to deliver an egg to the birthing hatchery. There they were stored until a child was needed to take the place of a death-rest. A father was chosen and the two tended the birthing chamber.

"Since the Collective has come, none have gone hungry or been sent to the cold north to live. Life is more boring but also much more comfortable."

We were interrupted by some of the males who landed among us and invited us to go swimming in a cavern.

"I would swear that a knowing looked passed between Crystal and Swane, her Mother, the woman who had been talking to us," I told Christie. Often I looked for the woman again and even questioned Crystal.

"She went on a Safari to the Northland. She gets bored. Says life is too easy now. She'll get tired of the cold and be back soon. I'll tell her you're looking for her."

"Maria is teaching me to sew like you Earthlings. Your earth flowers are much like ours." She sounded so sweet and innocent that I turned back to her questions about the flora of earth. Just as any other child away from home, I loved remembering, and for a moment in time, I was back in my Mother's rose garden. When I reconsidered the incident, I felt I was missing something I should have caught.

Ripple went to get the transport while Jazz got in my way helping me shower and adjusted the drying breeze slats on my body. Suddenly, he stood gazing at me. I looked deep into his eyes. It was as though his mind said to mine, "Don't go." Then, closed off again.

I looked at him closely. "Jazz, did you say something? Is everything all right?"

Jordan signaled from below that he and Ripple, as well as his harem, were ready. We dove off the deck of my cage, and swan dived to the waiting transport. Christie and her two escorts were a bit late but soon landed gracefully by our sides. We had been given flat rubber-soled sandals which absorbed some of the extra weight of our landings. All of us had lost weight on the delicate food supply available to us on the planet. We had plenty of food on board but the pods had such lovely delicious spices and variety of flavors that we preferred them.

The Captain, who was only allowed off ship half-time, and four crew members who were never allowed to intermingle with alien beings, began to look awkward and fat to us. Each of us was required to spend six hours per day on board ship. It was like 'island fever' on earth.

People who lived on an island often became so attached to it that they would not leave. In Old Canada, it was required that they leave the islands once a week and visit the mainland. We had such lovely times on Fairyland that we hated to return to the ship. It felt very confining.

Often at first, we found excuses to be late but soon gave it up when our Captain would impose a twenty-four penalty and we had to remain on the ship.

The environmentalist's designers had made our spaceship as earth-like as possible. We had gardens, forests, and pools. The ship light was close to natural, but the airy, clear brightness of this planet was a dream comes true. I wanted to stay here. Jazz and Ripple encouraged this longing. We were all invited to come and live on the planet, give up our travels, or return when we had finished our designated assignment of exploration. For the first time, I lost some of my dedication.

"Its puppy love and the eroticism of a different kind of lovemaking," the Captain said in my weekly hour of analysis.

"I feel its tug, also. I'm considering making you all return to the ship to rest. How much sleep are you really getting there? This isn't a party. It's a dedicated scientific effort. Don't forget to study your emotional and body reactions as well as the outside appearances of these lovely creatures."

This was the first time I had actually detected any emotion that was not positive.

I managed to sit by Christie. While the others were chatting, I asked her if she had felt any of this.

"Only the last week," she replied. Ripple bent his head over and kissed me, rubbing my arm. I knew he deliberately interrupted our communication.

Their transport was swift and silent. Only a couple of dials were set on the map dash board. The rest of the trip was on auto pilot, or so we had been led to believe. I had a sense of part of Ripple's mind controlling the ship, but shrugged it off. We did have mind controlled computers but only specially trained people on Earth used them. The captain had a certain amount of the ability, but this vehicle was not a computer. Or was it? Was I really seeing what was here, I wondered, or what I was used to seeing in my own environment?

Suddenly, I realized both Jazz and Ripple were gazing at me intently.

"Watch it." I heard Christie think-talk. When I looked at her however, she was smiling up at her comrade and then turned to Jordan to point out the change in the surface below. It looked like snow. We must be near their northern pole, I thought, deliberately breaking off my mind probe of Ripple.

"Do you ski here?" I asked brightly. "We wear two flat pieces on our feet and slide over the slick surface of the snow on earth. It's a bit like flying. I'll bet if I jumped off one of your mountains in your light gravity field, I could fly."

"Well, let's land and try it." Jazz said.

"Oh, no, Lorna, don't get them started," Jordan said. "We have to be ship side in two hours."

"I know. How about tomorrow? Can we come back this far and go skiing? I'm sure we have a couple of pair on board ship."

"Let's wait and see," said Jazz.

Again I glanced at him. Caution was not usually in his book.

What is in store for us? For the first time I wondered if we were in danger.

Jazz reached over and took my hand. "Are you all right, my coaszee?" It was an affectionate term that equated to our 'darling.'

"Oh, yes. Just excited about our adventure, I guess. I can hardly wait."

"You don't have to. We're here." Ripple called out. The transport hovered and lowered itself to the ground gently.

CASSADY'S TREASURE

I guess you might say I'm the bastard daughter of Butch Cassidy or the Sundance Kid, his best friend. Mother wasn't certain, but since Butch sent her money from time to time, she chose him. She laughed at rumors saying he had treasure stashed away in Bryce Canyon, Utah. They had simply retired to a ranch near Moab, Utah and changed their names.

When Mother died, Cassidy and Sundance invited me to spend some time with them at the ranch.

"Yippee," I shouted when I read the telegram.

At long last my dreams were about to come true. I bought myself a Stetson, a pair of cowboy boots, a six-shooter and headed west. If anyone thought a forty-year old woman looked funny in that get-up, he was wise enough to keep their mouths shut. I was wise enough to keep my jacket over the pistol.

All during my childhood, I had played at being a bank and train robber. When I arrived at womanhood, my resentment at being female filled me with depression.

Like mother, I became a schoolmarm, but unlike mother, I met no romantic bank robbers, or men who could hold a candle to my fathers. At night I dreamed of flickering campfires, shadowed figures, whispered conspiracies. The backfiring of exhausts were always gun battles. In my daydreams I was a Robin Hood bandit and my companions were Sundance and Butch. The Badlands were my dream home. If mother had not kept a close reign on me, I might have succeeded.

My visit to the ranch never terminated. Their home became mine. Both men were age-worn. The sands of time blew across the front porch as I listened to their tales of adventure over and over again.

"Remember South America?" one would begin.

The other would chuckle and say, "Tell her about it." Then continue the story himself until interrupted with a correction or addition by the other. Like fish tales they grew more sensational with each telling. Mother's version had been more conservative. They might pause and gaze wistfully into the night until I urged them to continue.

There was always an affectionate, intimate quality in the air when they spoke of her. The woman I had known as Mother became a beautiful heroine.

"She would glide into a bank or palace like a queen. Every head in the place would turn while she dropped packages and showed a bit of ankle, laughed and blushed. We took the money and were often gone before anyone realized what had taken place. She would melt into the crowd, throw a cloak over her shoulders, change into a cowboy cap and swagger off to an alley where we waited. By the time a posse got started we were home reading a book by the fire."

"Your Maw set a heap of store in books," was the way they would say it. "Guess it was her teacher ediekation. When she couldn't get us to read, she'd set us down and read to us. She never knowed we was jest enjoyin' lookin' at her and the sound of her voice." Then they laughed as though they had really fooled her.

I laughed along with them. If they put their mind to it, they could speak the King's English very well, but they had changed their names and enjoyed the many roles they'd played over the years. Now they were playing the role of retired, uneducated ranchers. No one except me knew they were the notorious couple.

Sometime Phillip would chime in and add to Cassidy's words, or each would tell the same tale differently. They laughed about their different ways of seeing things. It seemed OK that each had a different viewpoint.

I often pondered the ability of three people to love and cherish one another without jealousy. Each was very different. Their total acceptance of one another must account for it, I thought.

Mother never tried to hide anything from me. She loved them both and explained, "I took turns spending nights with each of them. At first it was thrilling, but eventually, it became too frustrating."

The men had been close friends nearly all their lives. Apparently, the only time they might have had a conflict was when both fell in love with the same woman. She was funny, intelligent and lovely. They finally agreed to live as a threesome.

But Mother was creative and needed to be alone often. Two men demanded too much of her time. Since she couldn't choose without breaking up their friendship and their way of life, she decided to go back east. I'm certain my impending birth helped her make the decision.

Philip, or The Sundance Kid, gentled down into a kind, sweet man. He would tell me tales about he and Butch that were funny and crazy. They would pull all kinds of stunts when robbing a stage or train. Sometimes giving money to a passenger who seemed in need.

When they spoke of Mother I hoped I was like her, but I was sure I lacked her beauty and sense of humor. They were very affectionate to me. Sometimes they looked at me strangely, as though seeking her in me. I had her smooth brow, freckled nose, light complexion, eyes like Butch and hair the coloring of Philips as a young man. Perhaps all of us speculated upon who my father really was, but as a whole, it didn't matter too much.

From Moab, Utah near the Colorado River, it was only a short ride to the exotic arched, rainbow bridges. Each year we rode up into the lovely, orange monuments and spent many days camping and hiking. I was no longer young myself the last time we went.

Once again they showed me how, if you stood in one arch, you could look through another arch and see blue sky. One was shaped like a bird and the other space was shaped like a half moon.

Sometimes Butch and I went alone. Philip would go when he felt strong enough.

Philip grew weaker and died first. Butch or Bruce as he neighbors knew him, died within a year. It was as though part of his spirit was gone. On his deathbed, Butch handed me the riddle to his treasure.

Road a horse to Moab, Utah,

Cross the desert's long back bone,

Past green rivers, rocks that balance,

As I enter Eden's throne.

Secret gardens, secret windows,

Double view, half moon and bird.

From an arch looking to heaven,

See a crack where eagles fly.

Cast a rope 'cross rocky rainbow,

Climb to top where eagles rest.

Under stone find rusted treasures,

Carry it back home tonight.

Now, I'm an old lady. What do I need with more money? I've decided this Halloween to give the world a treasure hunt. Yes, I know where the treasure lies and what he did at night when he thought I was asleep under the monuments.

It's yours if you can find it.

Good hunting, I'm going to bed.

A would-be bank robber.

PRINCE OF THE WIND
& BROKEN STICK

"Prince of the Wind. It is a proud and lofty name, is it not?" The old man raised his head proudly, and then took pity upon the young boy. He patted his shoulder.

The boy shrugged away the strong hand even though he knew the man meant to comfort him. The young Indian lad turned his face away from the wise Sachem. He was ashamed of his tears. For many years he had wanted to be like the Prince of the Wind, free, brave, and admired by all, but with a name like Broken Stick, who would take him seriously?

"How do I get a new name?" He finally asked.

"Each title in the tribe is earned in some way. A name can be changed if a person does a great act of heroism, or an important incident is attached to the person. A bit of the history of the people is passed on by the label earned. Sometimes desire, kindness, knowledge, work or strength alone can change a name, my son."

Broken Stick looked up at him questioningly.

"What would you like to be called? Write the name here." The old man pointed to the dark brown earth at his feet.

"What brave act have you done which might help you find another name? The old man continued.

"When I was a child I loved the wind, so I was called Windy until I earned a name. At the white man's school, they giggled at the name."

He paused, frowned at Broken Stick for a moment when he saw the grin on his face, then laughed aloud.

"One day our teacher, Mrs. Laughing Wolf, read us a story about a Prince who was strong, handsome and brave and a lovely maiden, Cinderella. Prince sounded like an important person. I liked the sound of it. P R I N C E...

The next day when the teacher called the roll, I said proudly, "I have chosen to be called Prince."

A second grader taunted me, "Prince? A Prince has to have a kingdom, Windy. Where is your kingdom? Or are you a Princess?"

Mrs. Laughing Wolf smiled and tipped her head as she looked at me. I stood before her. My anger and pride slowly turning to shame.

"Prince Windy. Prince of the Wind. What an exciting kingdom."   Prince of the Wind, she wrote in the book, erasing the old Windy.

"I felt like a great Chief. But I did not to get off so easily."

"By Friday, I want you to come before the class, tell us about your kingdom, where the wind roams, what it sees, who it touches and most importantly, what you feel about the wind."

"All week I ran in the wind, slept on a windy mountain top, saw it's effect on a rippling pond, the strength with which it bent a tree, a bird riding it's unseen force, and how it reshaped the earth, and people bending into it, I began to feel one with it.

"By Friday, I was full of stories about the wind, my kingdom. Not only could the wind be a gale, snowstorm, typhoon, a blizzard, it could be gentle and sweet. It could turn sand into a corkscrew, spiral upward, twist, bend, curve, meander and zigzag. I loved the sound of words to describe the wind and kept looking for more. I was so enthused, the class applauded. That is how I became a storyteller to my people and over the years earned the name, Prince of the Wind."

Broken Stick leaned against the knee of Prince of the Wind and nodded thoughtfully.

COON HUNTIN'

Hill men take a heap-of-pride in their hound dogs. Often they train them to hunt coons at night. Sometimes....well, sometimes things don't turn out well...Based on a true hunt.

A fiendish storm brewed above the lonely cabin in the Smoky Mountains of West Virginia. Marybelle could feel it in her bones. Even inside the cozy cabin she sensed it's brooding. Her twin sons, Mike and Ike came nosily home from school stomping the snow from their boots just outside the door.

"Reckon you boys better call off the coon hunt tonight. There's a storm brewin.' Hit's a mean one, too, or my nose ain't long fer nothin."

"Ah, Maw. We ain't afeared of no storm. If'n we're goin' ter be in the school Christmas Play, Mike and me plan ter have us some new shoes."

"Yeah, you can use a pair too, Maw." Mike came over to the rocking chair where she sat by the fire working on a quilt. He leaned over, pinching the toe sticking out the side of her worn shoe. They laughed as she giggled, then put her hand over her nose and mouth.

"Why don't you burn them stinkin' coats. You smell like a couple of skunks."

"If'n we was to go huntin' smellin' like a couple of city slickers, we'd come home with an empty poke."

"Ellen's comin' fer supper. Maybe her Pa, too. Don't be fergitten." Her cheeks had a warm glow and her eyes held a new sparkle.

The boys laughed again. El's Pa, George, was as sweet on their Maw as they were on Ellen, his lively, redheaded daughter.

"You want us to do the milkin' first?"

"No, you boys go on. Better give up the coon huntin.' Just check the traps and git on back home. Don't let that coon hound lead you into the storm. It's purty near dark already. Reckon I can still milk a cow, even if I am pushin 40 years come next month. You can fill the woodbox a'fore ye leave."

"We already did, Maw. We'll check the traps and be back 'fore you can say 'scat.'"

Marybelle watched her twin sons, Ike and Mike put on their coon skin caps, pick up their guns and walk out into the gray twilight. In the winter the days are too short, she thought.

A worried look came into her eyes. Wrapping her shawl around her shoulders she followed them onto the porch. A light snow was beginning to fall. The wind howled and tugged at her clothing.

Old Bess, the hound dog, danced around their feet. Each lad paused and scratched her ears, then she was off like a shot.

"Go get 'em Tiger," Ike yelled.

She watched as the hound circled the edge of the clearing looking for an animal trail to follow. Ike and Mike headed toward the creek to check their traps. At the bend they turned and waved to their mother.

The hound started baying when it found a fresh trail and all three went racing up the holler along the creek.

Marybelle felt a shiver of dread move through her body. Must be the cold. She went quickly back inside the cabin.

The large room had a fireplace at one end and a cook stove at the other. There was a curtain on the side where her bed could be sectioned off for privacy. The boys slept in the loft.

Marybelle and Tom, her husband, had built the cabin in the hills when they were married. They intended to add onto it after the twins were born, but Tom stepped on a rusty nail and died from blood poison.

Her mind roamed back over the past as though trying to hide from the storm which was beginning to roar and whistle around the cabin.

Tom and Marybelle's families had been on opposites sides in a blood feud. Merry, as Tom called her, fell in love and were meeting in secret. A jealous girl told both families. They tracked the couple to their rendezvous and shooting began. Marybelle and Tom were the only two left when the fued was over.

At the funerals, they stood on opposite sides of the cemetery, each with a gun in his hand. As the neighbors shoveled dirt into the holes, they looked at one another across the graveyard.

Tom raised his gun. Marybelle raised hers. Then, he threw his into the open grave at his feet. For a moment she hesitated, his handsome face in her sights. Merry's body sagged, she dropped the gun into her father's grave and fell to the ground weeping.

Her lover and worst enemy quickly covered the space between them. He took her in his arms and carried her to the buggy. They drove to a church where the preacher married them. Next day they loaded their meager belongings into a wagon and moved to the hills. Neither of them spoke of the past again.

Why am I thinking of it now, Merry wondered.

She went to the window. The snow had increased. George and El wouldn't come in this storm.

The tinkle of the cow bell reminded her she hadn't slopped the hogs or milked. It was already dark. Lighting both lanterns, she hung one on the porch and took the other with her to the barn to do the chores.

Milking the cow had always been a pleasure for her, especially on a cold evening. The warm body of the cow as she leaned against it, and fresh scent of milk, were comforting.

The cow, too, seemed to enjoy their little talks.

"They shoulda' been back by now. I reckon' I was an idiot to let them go, Jers. Lord knows I had me a feelin.' Ternight's a bad night. Course, they're purty near growed up. Have to make their own decisions some time. They be sixteen next month. Seems like yesterday they was new born colts.

"I'm right proud of them. Their Paa would be, too. Stand still, Jers. You're restless ternight. They shoulda' been back by now," she repeated with a frown and a worried tone.

The cow looked around at Marybelle. She wasn't Merry tonight. The animals shifted restlessly in their stalls. Goblin, the plow horse was due to give birth anytime.

"Hope you don't pick tonight to give us a colt." Merry stroked her sleek hide for a moment, picked up the pail of warm milk and went back to the house. The snow was thick and the wind howled like a panther 'round the cabin. She looked hopefully for footprints on the front steps.

Mike and Ike checked the traps. Two beaver and one fox in them. Cheerfully, they baited and reset each trap. They threw handfuls of fresh snow at a tree, each other, or old Bess if she barked too much. Had a quick skate on a beaver pond and hardly noticed the storm.

"Let's go home. It's gettin' too dark," Ike suggested and Mike nodded in agreement.

Up on the hillside, Old Bess struck a fresh scent.

"No coons tonight, Bess. Git on back here," Mike yelled.

The snow filled any tracks made within minutes. Bess seemed insistent and excited. Then the snow became so thick the dog lost the scent and came trotting back to them.

Suddenly, she stiffened and raced into a clump of nearby trees, baying to let them know she'd found an animal.

"Maw would be right proud if we couched ourselves a bear," Mike shouted to Ike above the wind.

"Shore would. But this storm is something fierce. Reckon' we'd best turn back." Ike was the more cautious one of the two. "Besides, I'm cold. Got snow in me boots and down the back of me coat."

All at once the hound came yipping back out of the thicket and shot past them.

"Reckon' that a bear's chasing her, now. We'd best get out of here. Come on Mike."

They heard a crash in the bushes nearby. Both boys raised their guns. Before he could pull the trigger, the bear was on Ike. It roared and slapped with it's large flat paws knocking him backward into the snow. Ike screamed.

Mike peered through the darkness. Against the whiteness of the snow he could make out shadowed figures.

He shot at the large black shadow bending over Ike. Loaded his rifle and shot again. His fingers were numb with fear.

Finally, the bear rolled off Ike. It roared once and tried to get up. Then, with a whimper the bear slumped down beside Ike and lay still.

A terrible silence fell on Mike's ears. Wind tore the words from his cold lips and froze the tears on his cheeks.

"Ike, Ike. Are you all right? Talk to me. Ike," he wailed. In the darkness he could smell blood. There were dark splotches on the snow and sticky warm moisture on his hands when he touched Ike's body. "Oh, my God," he wept.

The snow became thinner and the air colder. Mike knew they would both freeze if they didn't get home soon. Throwing his gun aside he sat on the hillside. Using the gunnysack that held the beaver and fox, he managed to tie his brother onto his back. They slid and rolled down the ridge to the meadow.

When the dog came bounding against the door, Marybelle let her in. She thought the boys would be close behind and pushed supper from the warm side of the stove to the hot side. Then Bess wanted out again.

By the time Mike came to the little creek that flowed down the holler past the cabin, his legs were so cold he could hardly bend them. Tears froze on his face and the ice nearly blinded him. His hands were numb. He could not tell if he was holding on to Ike or not.

Often when they approached the house the boys yodeled to let their Mother know they were home. Then, they did the chores or skinned out the coon and animals from the traps before going inside.

There was a faint light ahead. He had to get Ike home.

He tried to yodel for help. "Yodaleelle, yodalee.." The listening Mother heard the faint call. Her heart was thankful. She waited. The boys often yodeled when they came back, then went to the barn to skin the animals.

She thought Old Bess had rushed out to meet the boys and was surprised when she came back, sat on the porch and howled.

Bess is acting strange, Marybelle thought, reminding herself the boys had yodeled and they were home.

Old Bess howled again. Marybelle grabbed a shawl and lantern and went to meet her sons.

On the porch was a large frozen bundle. Mike had made it home with Ike still tied to his back.

She tried to pull them through the doorway, but they were frozen together and covered with icy snow. They were too wide to fit through the door. Cutting the gunnysack with a knife, her fingers icy, she found they were still frozen together.

Finally, she put her bedding on them and sat by the open door all night.

In the morning, Old Bess had crawled in beside them. She too died, as though in shame for having abandoned them when the bear chased her.

BONDAGE

Egon chafed under the bondage of a storm-trap of his own making. This white man's shack reeked of shadowed loneliness. The tallow candle flickered; the only movement besides his own. He lifted his bulky form and kicked aside a kaleidoscope, game toys and many other things he's spent his hide money on last summer.

Mother had warned him, "You are a child and buy toys. A man buys knives, fishhooks, builds a boat, finds a wife to keep him warm in the winter and bear sons."

"Anyone can have a wife," he grumbled and stuffed his catalog in his pocket. The octagon kit he'd ordered and put together for a house looked great in the summer, but he'd had to cover it with ice blocks and remove the door to turn it back into the snug, protective igloo of his people. Even yet, the ceiling was too high. There was too much air space to keep warm.

He opened the worn catalog and peered at a pair of snowshoes. If only he had bought them instead of toys. Games were not much fun when played alone. If he had those snowshoes he could go see his family, even in the sobbing storm howling around his walls. He pulled furs closer over his shoulders and lay back, closing his eyes against the candlelight casting sinister shadows of loneliness.

Egon dreamed. He swam with seals. His grandfather caught him in a net and pulled him into a boat. For Christmas that year, Grandfather had made him a pair of snowshoes. He'd been so proud of them.

"But of course." Egon sat up. "I'll make my own snowshoes." He pulled out his knife, lifted a hide from the floor and began cutting it in strips. Outside a wolf howled. Even if he made the shoes, would he be able to make it past the wolves? He shoved the strips aside and hugged his knees, but the mother lode of tapped imagination committed him to action. A burning desire for company drove his fingers as he carved frames from boards of his octagon home.

At first his fingers, weaving the leather, fumbled awkwardly. Slowly, his ancestral mind-map remembered the path of weaving. He became so absorbed in the snowshoe project he forgot to be bored. With reluctance, he paused to chew on dried bear meat and a bit of fish. It's as thought there's a pencil in my mind, he thought, and my fingers are learning to follow it's lines.

Heavy weights lifted from his spirit. He no longer felt pinched between the past and future. Egon sat for a long time thinking about the anticipation of buying bright new toys and their brief moments of enjoyment. Weighing it against the pleasure of making something himself, he realized their gloss had hidden his own talents.

The weaving of the snowshoes was so engrossing he almost let the candle burn out. That night he lay back. His fingers ached from the threading and pulling, the knot tying of leather thongs. The ache was well earned. Tomorrow he would try out his handiwork.

Outside the storm roared threateningly, a wolf howled. Egon he smiled. He was no longer a slave to the elements. "I'll make a spear tomorrow and perhaps after that, a boat, a wife. . ."

THE IN'S AND OUT'S OF DREAMING

Father McDodger, the priest, stood outside the pearly gates for the second time,

The first time he had been certain he would gain entrance. Hadn't he, after all, been priest to the President of the greatest country in the world?

"Your life is a draw," said the Ultimate Judge as he stood before His Throne. "You are neither good enough to go to Heaven or bad enough to go to Hell."

"Wasn't trying to saving the President's life a beneficent act of ultimate goodness?" the priest asked.

"Or was it a selfish act?" Asked the Judge. "Think on it. Each person has the final answer to the quality of his life in his own heart. No one enters The Gate until a thorough, self-evaluation of his life-long acts has been made. Go, think, and pray. Because you have tried to be a Godly man on earth, after you have reached a decision, you will have a chance to re-enact your final sacrifice, if you choose to do so."

The priest awoke in his chair. Looking around himself, he saw a richly furnished office. Gifts from the President and Government officials from many countries surrounded him. Inlaid tables, silver, paintings, rugs, and this beautiful mahogany desk. Father rubbed his hand across its satin surface fondly, Then paused, remembering.

The President had given him this desk after he had gone on public Television and agreed that the President's latest aggressive action against a small impoverished country was done in order to save the world from Communism.

"God is on the side of your President, my people," his powerful bass voice had rung out across the stadium. Father was not only blessed with a voice that could say, 'Pardon me, which way to the outhouse?' and people would applaud, but he was a tall, strikingly handsome person with a brilliant, kindly smile, 'An Eisenhower' smile, his Mother had called it.

Father remembered the dream, He paused as he pondered its meaning, It had seemed so real.

The day, this day, was the 4th of July. The President had given the usual short address about patriotism and Father Dan had blessed the people and the holiday. Soon the world renowned fireworks above the White House Lawn would be launched.

As usual, when Cynthia and little Dan were not with the President, a chant went up, "We want Cynthia, we want Daniel, we want Cynthia..."

Where were they? Father Dan wondered for a moment and then remembered that from some vague fear, he had asked Cynthia not to come. She had laughed at him but promised. John did not seem concerned about their absence as he stood back from the microphones and waved at the crowds.

The President was standing by Dan's side telling him about his Sunday afternoon golf game while the crowd applauded and chanted. A woman, dressed as a White House Aide, approached Father Dan and kissed his ring. Then, reaching into her purse, she pulled a gun and turned toward the President. Father saw there was also a small bomb in her open handbag.

Quickly, he grabbed the purse and reached for the gun. Father Dan had been shot. He remembered the confusion, an ambulance, and the hospital. Then, the President standing over his bed, Cynthia crying, and little Daniel's tearful request, "Please don't be sick Father."

Camera's clicked around them. Johnny, the President, never let anything go by that would make good publicity. Sometimes Father wondered if he would have allowed the reporters into his bedroom if it would have led to another vote.

After that, there was a soft light feeling and he found himself standing before a set of white Pearly Gates wondering how they opened. Then the iridescence presence of a Judge flowed like a cool breeze across his emotions. In his heart, Father McDodger understood that his actions on Earth had been questionable,

It was a surprise when he realized it was only a dream, but it was such a haunting dream, Dan continued to re-evaluate his life. There was a scent of light perfume in the air. Had Cynthia been here and found him asleep?

He smiled a bit cynically as he thought of Cynthia, She scorned the President's bed but loved the importance of being in partnership with the person in power over the most advance technological country in the world. Cynthia had agreed not to ask for a divorce or talk about her husband's sexual deviations, provided she have a full hand to discuss issues, travel, and take advantage of any opportunities she saw fit to use.

She was an intelligent capable woman and would have made a better President than her husband. Father McDodger often accompanied her on trips to the United Nations. Eleanor Roosevelt and Cynthia would have made an unbeatable pair. She might compromise on some areas but on equal rights, one world, a clean earth, education and welfare, she stood firm. Father felt her proposed programs were beginning to make progress. Due to television, she was one of the most popular figures on Earth.

Father Dan leaned back in his chair. Tears slipped beneath his closed eyelids as he remembered the three young, innocent children who had been born so long ago in a wealthy suburb in Washington.

"Were we so wrong in trying to work within the framework of our lives and our human weakness to improve conditions in the world? If we had worked from impoverishment and weakness, could we have accomplished anything?" Father Dan wondered aloud.

He remembered the life of Christ. Perhaps, he thought, but...He shook his head and continued to visualize the three of them and attempt to discover where they could have changed their lives.

Cynthia Hartly, Dan McDodger, and John Lincoln had been neighbors in a wealthy district in Washington, DC With a name like Lincoln in Washington, where could John go but politics? Johnny's father was an Ambassador.

Both of the boys were in love with Cynthia. She seemed to enjoy their company. Johnny had charm, a great sense of humor and a gift of gab that would eventually enable him to become a successful lawyer and politician. Dan believed Cynthia preferred John so went with them when invited and never tried to date her. He was simply a friend who escorted Cynthia when Johnny was not available. Dan was a tall, gangly teenager with a bad case of acne. His voice boomed and his large hands always seemed to be in the way, John must have seen the potential in him, or Dan made him seem self-assured and sophisticated in comparison in those days. Whatever the reason, Dan had been grateful to have such popular intelligent friends his own age.

Dan's mother died when he was in High School. After this, his Father treated him as a friend, confidant, and an adult. Dan's Father coordinated a large section of Department of Health, Education and Welfare,

The weight of the decisions of the department rested heavily on the head of this conscious stricken man. He would talk with Dan for hours about the fact that there was so much food available and government red tape wasted it, or made profit by it. His branch of government contained dozens of little departments, each with a power hungry head who acted as though he was God. Actually, the little power each had added up to enough to foul up simple actions and starve half of the world.

During the years following college, Dan saw little of Cynthia, Johnny, as John Lincoln was called in high school, went to Georgetown University with Dan so they saw one another often,

Dan remembered when Johnny and Cynthia had an argument at the Senior Prom and she stormed home.

"What was that all about?" Dan had asked Johnny.

At first she had written and called often.

Cynthia confided that she was engaged to someone she had met at college. She married at the end of the year but continued school in another state.

Dan's Father became ill and died at Christmas time just before graduation, After his father's death, he felt so alone, The fellowship of the Church became his sanctuary.

The next summer, Johnny went on a trip with his father to South Africa. One of the priests at college began to talk with Dan about joining the priesthood.

When he saw Johnny again, he was swinging between fast women, drink, and young boys and girls alike, The underlying corruption in his surrounding made Dan long for the dreamed of quiet and peaceful retreat that the monks offered, Cynthia was happily married he supposed.

Upon graduation, Dan became a priest and saw little of his friends,

After ten years of trying to bind up the wounds of the poor and afflicted, John began to develop the same type of cynicism that his Father had felt, Often when he aided a woman, whether to comfort her or help her make a better life for himself, she inevitably made a pass at him, sometimes the men did too, Real financial aid was hard to obtain,

Dan felt powerless to help more than a few at a time, It was the priests with the large parishes that had access to

Church funds and positions that could make a change in both Church and State.

By the age of Thirty five, Dan began to look in the mirror and like what he saw, The booming rusty voice of an insecure young man had become well-modulated in tone. People liked to listen to the sound of it, His quiet ways made him seem wiser than he probably was.

When Dan decided to move up in the Church, the old political maneuvering from the past was already known from the political days with his Father. He decided to put this knowledge to use effectively. Between that, the priesthood itself, and his charm, he moved swiftly to gain the power he needed to improve the world.

Cynthia's husband, father and mother were killed in a plane crash. Dan was asked to conduct the services. John came to the funeral.

After that, the three of them began to get together for dinner, help one another in their careers and life in general. Johnny had a divorce behind him, They had all settled down a great deal and wanted to see a better world for themselves and others. All three were working in the Washington area.

John was running for the Senate. Cynthia had decided to go into politics as well. Dan and she agreed to help John with his campaign. He in turn would help her get an appointment to a post at the United Nations,

"Just like Eleanor Roosevelt," John laughed as he told Dan about it.

"Just like Eleanor Roosevelt," commented Cynthia with a proud tilt to her chin. Father Dan felt a tightening in his chest, but he had long ago resigned his feelings for Cynthia to a quiet acceptable shelf inside his heart. He decided love without possession enriched his spiritual life.

About two month's before his election to the Presidency, Johnny and Cynthia came to Dan. They told him they had decided to become partners in politics and wanted him to become their third partner. Johnny and Cynthia would get married and present the family image that seemed so important to voters. A trusting friend who was a priest would be an additional vote getter. They would both work as hard as John. All profits, above expenses, would be split three ways. Each would help promote the causes the other felt important in his life's work.

"We have known each other all our lives," John said. "If we can trust anyone, it is one another. Cynthia wants a career with the United Nations but she's starting late, this will put her near the top. You want to be able to make your church change some policies and enact some reforms. Who will they listen to? The priest for the President of the United States."

At his questioning look, Cynthia nodded. "We intend to build a solid triangle. Who knows politics better than the three of us? We're intelligent and reasonably honest people. I feel the United Nations should be strengthened and the United States needs to give more than just financial support. I want the power to make a difference in the world."

"What do you want John?" Dan asked looking him directly in the eye? More young men?"

"I am into psychoanalysis and have promised to stick to the female sex and to Cynthia to be true." He took her hand and she smiled into his eyes, not a loving smile but a knowing sexual one. Dan turned away, but he knew Cynthia's searching glance caught the pain before he could cover it.

She came to him and put her arm around his waist. "I won't go into this thing if you refuse, Dan," she said softly. "You're already married to the church."

Was that my first big compromising act, Dan wondered?

He was too intelligent to blame anyone but the weakness of his own flesh and mind. Over the years, the Big Three, as the press called them, could do no wrong in the people's eyes.

But underneath, John had managed to gain too much influence over the worlds good. Cynthia had made great reforms in the United Nations. In fact, she would probably soon become the new Secretary General. She was thrilled at last be in a position to follow through on some the new rules and programs she had help write and support.

"Now if John will follow through on his promises, perhaps we can make a better world," she told Dan.

It would put her in opposition to many of the things John stood for. Dan could feel the strong partnership of the years coming apart at the seams. Both Cynthia and John could become ruthless when they desired a thing.

At times that seemed to be the only way to get things done. Dan had applied some of the same tactics to his own order and had received gratifying results, except for his own conscious.

Father Dan continued to sit at the desk with his feet on it, his hand clasped and his head tilted forward. He was thinking of the dream message in relation to his own life.

"Darling, there you are," Cynthia floated in, coming around the desk and kissing him on the lips, "What is it Dan? You seem so far away."

He stood up, took her arms in his hands, and looked into her blue-green eyes, "Cynthia, please don't go to the ceremony today. Please."

"Dan, let loose, you're hurting me." He released her and she stepped backward.

Then she took his arm and led him to a soft couch. "Sit down and tell me about it. What is it? What do you know?"

"Well, I had this strange dream. It was so real. Someone tried to kill Johnny." Dan faltered. He knew how weak it sounded.

"Oh, just a dream. You're too old for dreams, Dan, unless they're about me," she said leaning over and kissing him lightly on the cheek. "Besides, do you think it would be an injustice if John was killed? Let's face it, indirectly, he's probably killed more people than Hitler, all in the name of God and Justice."

She was serious and Dan nodded in agreement. He stood up slowly, like an old man,

"Come on, darling. We both know that life is never fair. If it had been, you and I would have been married and had a dozen kids by now, just like the Kennedy's. But I couldn't see past a case of acne, or Johnny's deceiving smile. You couldn't see past your dreams and Johnny can't see past his penis, unless there's power involved. We turned out to be just like everybody else in the world didn't we? But, should we really be disappointed in ourselves for being human after all?"

Cynthia had a quick mind and a way with words. Dan paced the floor. "Really, Dan, This evening isn't the time for stewing about your dreams. You remind me more of your Father every day. Now go shower and change, You look as though you slept in that chair. Hurry. In fifteen minutes and we're suppose to go to dinner and then the firework's ceremony.

"Cynthia, please? Promise me you won't bring little Daniel to the platform tonight? Watch from your balcony and I'll join you there to watch the fireworks after the speeches."

She looked long and hard at this man she had loved for so many years. He asked very little of her. Finally, she relented. "OK, Dan. This once, but little Daniel will be disappointed. We'll watch out the nursery window. Come and join us as soon as you can get away."

"Thanks Cynthia. For the first time in years, he reached out for her, took her in his arms and held her close to him. When he released her and stepped back, she saw the tears in his eyes,

Cynthia hesitated knowing he was not going to give her any more information at the moment. Perhaps he couldn't or it was just a disturbing dream as he had said.

Again she gave him a quick hug, and shook her head as she left the room. He watched her long slim legs in silver nylons and let his eyes travel up her soft body to the auburn hair coiled on top with a silver clasp holding it smoothly together.

Of all the things he had done in life, his most precious memory was of the week they had spent alone together on the lake four years earlier. Johnny had called saying that he would be late. Dan and Cynthia should map out the strategy of the campaign and the general outline their speeches should cover in each area. It would be a week at least before he could join them.

They had done it all before, but this one was for his second term as Presidency. If all went well in the second term, John was determined he would be the first President since Roosevelt to have a third term. A rule for Johnny was always there to be challenged and broken.

"He's probably holed up with some new young man," Cynthia said bitterly.

"I'm sorry Cynthia."

"I'm not. Disappointed a bit. John is a brilliant man and his intentions toward me are respectful but whether you admit it or not, Dan, the reason both of us went along with Johnny was mainly so we could be together."

Dan looked at her in astonishment. Had it been so obvious?

"I think I've always loved you, Dan. It took me a long time to sort out the difference between lust and love. Johnny has the capacity to lust or to love but not both together. He loves us but if he could use us sexually, he would no longer care for us. Many people are like that. You love me, Dan, and I know you want me, but are you mature enough to experience the combination together?

"I know you've held back over the years because you might loose the benefit of the power of priesthood, I did not want to loose the power of being the second most influential person in the country, so I haven't pushed you.

"But just this once Dan, between you, me, and God, let there be honest emotion. Do you really believe that two people who genuinely love one another can be condemned for having a loving sexual encounter, when it is mankind's greatest joy and comfort? Dan's eyes glowed as they probed hers, seeking sensitivity and affirmation above the flow of her words.

"I would like to make you a proposition. We take this one week out of our lives and spend it together. Then, after this week, we sacrifice the sexual part of our lives, knowing we're giving up something precious to work for the projects in which we believe so strongly. If you will share this time with me, I will be your friend for life, Otherwise, I will know you for a coward who does not have the courage to taste life before he condemns it."

Dan stood looking for her for a long minute, thinking about her words. Then, he crossed the room and hungrily took her into his arms,

Suddenly, he knew why people married, loved, fought, and died together. He knew why they acted as though there was an invisible something out there worth fighting for.

Something men like Johnny was able to exploit but would never know. Yes, and men like himself.

The three had a drink together as they told Johnny of their pact. He said, with a touch of envy in his voice, "You're nuts. You'll never be able to go through with it."

But they had. Through it all, they had remained comrades. Even after little Daniel had been born nine months later

Oh, his arms often longed for Cynthia and he dreamed about her at night. He had a vision of what life could be for the average man and it tempered his actions toward others. Dan was not always innocent in his actions for good, but he did get reforms through. Life had been good to him in many ways, Johnny had accused him of becoming smug recently.

Now he wondered again, were he and the President really friends? Or had they simply been using one another and yes, even God for power all these years? Had he been right or weak in withholding his advise during crisis, in not speaking out when he had a chance against some of the Presidents programs for fear Johnny would not support his own pet projects?

Father Dan fell on his knees and hid his thoughts in prayerful repetitions.

An Aide called, "The President is waiting for you."

Dan walked down the long hallway of decision and joined the group of dignitaries who would share the platform for the Forth of July ceremonies.

He had missed dinner so Johnny introduced him to the few people he had not met. The priest shook hands with the heads of a dozen powerful nations.

As in the dream, he re-lived the scene again and knew that his final decision was at hand.

He saw the assassin and realized the explosives were hid in her purse. The pistol was in her hand.

This time, the priest did not deflect the bullets or snatch the purse that held the bomb. He had made a final decision.

This time, when he stood before The Ultimate Judge. would The Gates swing out or in?